D0995267

WITHDRAWN

Girlfriends

I expect probably this is where I ought to tell about us all. The four of us. Lily, Keri, Frizz and me. We've been friends since just about as long as I can remember. Since Reception! Well, we have known each other since Reception. Frizz and me started being best friends in Year Two, and Lily and Keri in Year Three. And then we all became best friends together. The Gang of Four! Lily 'n' Keri 'n' Frizzle 'n' me. Everybody knew us! Even the teachers. They knew we all sat together and did things together and stuck up for each other. When we left Juniors to go to different schools, we made this sacred solemn vow that we would stay friends for ever. Come what may, for better or for worse. We swore a special oath and sealed it with our own spit (instead of blood).

Also by Jean Ure
in the Girlfriends series

Pink Knickers Aren't Cool!
Girls Are Groovy!
Boys Are OK!

Orchard Black Apples

Get a Life
Just 16
Love is for Ever

ORCHARD BOOKS
338 Euston Road, London NW1 3BH
Orchard Books Australia
Hachette Children's Books
Level 17/207 Kent Street, Sydney, NSW 2000

ISBN 978 1 84616 963 2

First published in 2002 by Orchard Books
This edition published in 2008
A paperback original

A CIP catalogue record for this book is available from the British Library.

3 5 7 9 10 8 6 4
Printed in Great Britain

Orchard Books is a division of Hachette Children's Books,
an Hachette UK company

www.hachette.co.uk

Girls Stick Together!

JEAN URE

ORCHARD BOOKS

Chapter 1

Starting at a new school is definitely scary. Especially when you don't know anyone. Then it is *double* scary!

A week ago I'd gone with Mum to buy my uniform. I wasn't scared then. I was excited! The High School uniform is green kilts and waistcoats, or sweaters for when it's cold. Keri says that all uniforms are naff, and that the High School uniform is one of the naffest. I don't agree! I know that Keri is our Style Queen, and dead cool, and buys all her gear from this mega-trendy store called Go Girl that I have almost never got anything from, as Mum says it is way too expensive and she is not forking out a week's wages for something I will grow out of before she has time to turn round, but I *don't care*. I just happen to think that green kilts and waistcoats are neat. So there!

Anyway. We bought the uniform and as soon as I got home I tried it all on again – just in case they'd given us the wrong size, or something; it's always best to check – and Mum yelled upstairs, "Polly! Come down and show Mr Deacon!" So I went next door and did a bit of a twizzle for Mr Deacon who is old as old but still takes an interest in what me and Craig are up to.

Then Mum wanted to take photos to send to my grans, and then Dad arrived and said, "Hey, get a load of that! Give us a twirl then!" and as I was twirling Craig came clumping through the door, took one look and went, "Yuckaroony! Green grollies!"

He can talk! His school has purple blazers with *bright yellow stripes*! That is yuckaroony, if anything is. They look like piles of vomit, going down the road.

I said this to him, and Mum said, "Polly and Craig! Stop being so disgusting." But it is the way we talk to each other. We do it all the time. (Craig is my brother and older than me by eighteen months, though quite honestly he is so childish it is just unbelievable.)

I spent the whole of that week trying on my new uniform. I love it to bits! Frizz came round and wanted to see me in it. She said in wistful tones that she wished she could have a uniform like that. "Black is so grungy."

Black is what they wear at Heathfield.

"But green *kilts*," I said. "It's a bit yucky!"

"I don't think it's yucky," said Frizz. "I think it's nice."

I reminded her that Keri had said it was dead naff.

Frizz said, "Oh! Well. Keri."

I must admit that I giggled when she said this. As a rule we all agree, Frizz and me and Lily, that Keri is just so-o-o-o cool.

"Gives herself these airs and graces," said Frizz.

That is not at all a Frizz-type phrase. I reckon she'd heard her mum say it. Mums tend to think that Keri is a bit *too* cool. They would like us to stay ten years old for ever!

All week long I peacocked about in my uniform, trying it in all different ways. First with the waistcoat, then with the sweater. Then with the skirt normal length, then rolled over at the waist. Then with black tights, then with green. You can wear either. (But not brown, for some reason. Maybe Mrs Kershaw, the

Headmistress, has a thing about it.)

By Monday, which was the start of term, I was feeling quite used to my lovely green uniform. But now I was all shaky and scared about going somewhere new. I had hordes of butterflies swarming in my stomach. I could feel them, fluttering and flitting. Suddenly I wished more than anything that I was going to Heathfield, with Frizz. I wished Mum and Dad had never made me sit the scholarship. I wished I'd never passed.

I'd secretly been a bit proud when I'd first heard. I'd been a bit puffed up. Poor old Frizz, I'd thought, stuck at Heathfield! Boring black uniform. Huge classes. *Boys*. But at least Frizz would know people. There were loads of them going there from our old school. Practically half the class! And Lily was starting at Rosemount, which was where she'd always dreamed of going, and it wouldn't matter that she wouldn't know anyone because nobody else would either. They would all be new together. People come from all over, to go to Rosemount. It is a famous dance school and even has people from places such as Australia and Japan.

As for Keri, at her posh new boarding school, it wouldn't bother her one little bit. Keri isn't in the least shy. She just barges straight in and takes over. I wish I could be like that! But I am not, unfortunately. When I first meet people I am rather silly and turned in on myself.

I expect probably this is where I ought to tell about us all. The four of us. Lily, Keri, Frizz and me. We've been friends since just about as long as I can remember. Since Reception! Well, we have known each other since Reception. Frizz and me started being best friends in Year Two, and Lily and Keri in Year Three. And then we all became best friends together. The Gang of Four! Lily 'n' Keri 'n' Frizzle 'n' me. Everybody knew us! Even the teachers. They knew we all sat together and did things together and stuck up for each other. When we left Juniors to go to different schools, we made this sacred solemn vow that we would stay friends for ever. Come what may, for better or for worse. We swore a special oath and sealed it with our own spit (instead of blood).

Mum apologised for not being able to come with me, that first morning. She said, "I'm really sorry, Pol! I would if I could, but we're so short-handed."

She meant at work. She does care work at a local home for old people. I assured her that I really didn't mind going by myself. To be honest, I thought it would be a bit babyish, turning up with your mum. I'd been going to suggest that she dropped me off half a block early so no one would see us!

"I'll be all right," I told her.

"Perhaps you ought to go in on the bus with Craig," said Mum.

Go in with Craig? I recoiled, in horror. "*Mum*," I said, "I'll be all *right*!"

"Just this first morning," pleaded Mum. "So I can be sure that you get there. You know how daffy you are!"

Craig didn't like the idea any more than I did. He pointed out that in fact he got off two stops before me. "I'm not staying on just to take her in to school."

"No, no, no!" said Mum. "I'm not asking you to do that. Just make sure she gets the right bus. Just this once...for my sake. Humour me!"

So we humoured her. We went diddying up the road together, Craig in his vomity-striped blazer, me in my green grolly one. The top of the bus was full of other boys in vomity stripes, plus a few girls in grolly green.

Craig said, "There's your lot", and gave me a little push. What was I supposed to do? I didn't know any of them! He is just so yucky, my brother.

Actually, although it is true that I didn't know any of the girls on the bus, it is not quite true that I didn't know anyone at the High School. I knew Jessamy Jones.

Jessamy is this person that we were at Juniors with and that we didn't like very much as she is the most terrible show-off and boasts all the time about herself and her achievements. Frizz and the others had felt really sorry for me, that I was going to be stuck in the same school as Jessamy for the rest of my days. I had vowed that I would simply ignore her. As it happened, however, it was her that ignored me. Well, practically.

When I got to school, I was taken to this classroom and told to find myself a desk, which wasn't easy since most of them were already occupied. This was on account of me getting a bit lost on my way from the bus stop. I went and turned down the wrong road and didn't know where I was and had to ask this lady, which is the stupid sort of thing I am always doing. I just have no sense of direction. It is quite pathetic, and also a bit scary, especially when I fly into one of my panics as I did that first morning, thinking *help!* and *woe!* and will I ever get there?

If it hadn't been for the lady, I might not have done. I might still be out there, half way to Land's End!

Almost everyone else had already arrived. It was really embarrassing, having to search for an empty desk with all these pairs of eyes watching me. Then I saw Jessamy sitting in the back row, and it was just *such* a relief, I mean somebody I actually knew, even if it was only bossy old show-off Jessamy. Before I could stop myself I had broken into this beam and waved and said, "Hello!"

That horrible snotty girl! All she did was just stretch her lips ever so slightly, like about 0.2 of a millimetre, and in this very concentrated fashion she started picking tangles out of her hair. She yanked a strand of it in front of her face and peered at it, all up close, like she was looking for nits, or something. Talk about unfriendly! In the end, another girl took pity on me and called out that there was an empty desk next to her.

So I went and sat next to this other girl, who told me that her name was Lettice, which strikes me as a very odd kind of name to have. I mean, it's like being called Cabbage, or Turnip, or something. Fruits are all right. Well, there's Cherry; that's pretty. I have to say I've never heard of anyone called Apple or Banana. But Peach would be nice. Lettice is just *weird*.

Actually, she was quite a weird sort of girl, even if

she had taken pity on me. She looked a bit like a lettuce, sort of limp and soggy. She kept dabbing at me and saying stuff like, "Polly, it is Polly, isn't it? Let's stick together, just you and me, and never mind all that lot." I mean, I didn't yet know if I wanted us to stick together, though I was grateful to her for telling me about the desk.

Just as I thought everyone was there, the door opened again and another girl was brought in, and it was Chloë that had been at my interview. I was so pleased to see her! I'd often thought about her, and wondered if she'd got in. And she had!

She saw me, and grinned, and I grinned back. She looked just like I remembered her, with this little bright pointy face and sticky-out teeth, and dark hair cut short and ragged. All in spikes and spokes. Totally crazy! I grinned like mad and felt this great big warm splurge of happiness. Now that Chloë was here, I would have a friend.

There was only one empty desk left, and it was right down at the front, but it wasn't all that far away from me. I mean, easily within talking distance. But, oh! That hateful Jessamy! She obviously looked at Chloë and thought, "She looks like she could be popular." And then she realised that Chloë was a new girl and didn't know anyone, 'cos most of the others had come up from Juniors together, so guess what? She wangled it so that the girl in the desk next to her changed places with another girl, and the other girl changed places with Chloë, and Chloë ended up sitting *next to Jessamy*. It wasn't Chloë's fault; I mean, she didn't know what was going on. She just did what that bossy girl told her.

At breaktime, 'cos they were nearer the door than me, Jessamy rushed Chloë out into the yard before I even had a chance to speak to her, and she did the same at lunch time, too, so that by the time I got to the dining hall they were already at the head of the queue, and by the time I got my lunch they were sitting at a table with four other girls and there wasn't any room for me. Chloë pulled a sympathetic sort of face, as if it wasn't what she really wanted, but I'd got Lettice flapping about just behind me, and most probably, to be honest, it looked like her and me were bosom buddies.

Lettice *wouldn't* leave me alone. All the time she kept dabbing and patting and going, "Let's be friends! Just you and me." It was better than being on my own, but I wasn't awfully sure how much I liked her. I mean, she was OK, I didn't *not* like her. But I really wanted to be friends with Chloë!

At the end of the day I marched off to the bus stop, with Lettice flipping and flapping at my side.

"I don't really come in this direction," she puffed. "I live *that* way. But if we're going to be friends" – flip, flap – "we've got to do things together."

I just grunted, 'cos to tell you the truth I felt like running away and never coming back. I hated the High School! I hated Jessamy! I hated Lettice! I hated everyone!

"Tomorrow," panted Lettice, breathing down my ear, "*you* can walk with *me*." She hopped out into the gutter and back again. "We'll take it in turns! You come half way with me, I come half way with you. Right?"

I didn't answer her. Instead I screeched, "There's my bus!" and I ran.

Needless to say, the first thing Mum wanted to know when I arrived back was, "How did it go?"

I muttered that it was all right. I wasn't going to tell Mum that Jessamy Jones had ignored me and stopped Chloë being friends with me and that the only person who took any notice of me was a wet lettuce leaf. I mean, it was just too humiliating.

But Mum persisted. "How about that nice girl you

met at your interview? What was her name? Clara? Caroline?"

I snapped, "Chloë!"

"Chloë," said Mum. "That was it! Did she manage to get a scholarship?"

Reluctantly, I said, "Yes."

"Oh, that's wonderful," said Mum. "Are you in the same class?"

I nodded.

"So you can be friends. Isn't that lovely?"

"Mm," I said.

"Well, you might sound a bit more enthusiastic," said Mum. "I thought you liked her?"

I did like her! I felt my glasses begin to steam up. (Perhaps I should have said before that I wear glasses, but I am rather self-conscious about it.)

"Now where are you off to?" cried Mum, as I bolted out of the kitchen. Bundle, our dog, bolted with me, barking loudly as he did so.

"Going to ring Frizz!" I yelled.

"Well, don't be all day," warned Mum. "Tea's nearly ready!"

Frizz must have been practically sitting on top of her telephone 'cos she answered it immediately. "Polly! I was just going to ring you! I only just got in."

"Same here," I said.

Then there was this pause, and then we both spoke together. "So what was it like?"

Another pause.

"You first," I said.

Frizz heaved a sigh. She said that it was OK, but not the same without me and the others.

"It's worse for me," I said. "I don't know anyone!"

"You know Jessamy," said Frizz.

Jessamy! *YUCK*.

"What are you doing?" said Frizz.

I said, "I'm gnashing my teeth."

"Sorry!" Frizz gave this little apologetic cackle.

"Just do not *talk* to me" – I gnashed a bit more – "about *Jessamy Jones*."

"All right," said Frizz. She's ever so obliging. She always does what you tell her.

"So who are you going round with?" I said.

"Oh…" Frizz named two girls from our old school. Darcie White and Melanie Philpotts.

"*Darcie?*" I said. "And *Melanie?*"

"Well, just for the moment. I mean, we're not actual friends or anything." Frizz hastened to reassure me. "We just sort of…sit next to each other."

"They are so *dire*," I said. It wasn't that I was

jealous or anything. But really! I bared my teeth at the telephone. "Melanie *Philpotts*! Yuck!"

"Darcie's not that bad," said Frizz.

"Apart from being a total twonk," I said.

"Well." Frizz heaved another sigh. "You have to hang with someone. How about you?"

"Oh, there's this girl," I said airily. "Lettice. She wants to be friends with me. She's been sticking like glue."

"Lettice," giggled Frizz.

"That's her name."

"Funny sort of name."

"Yes. Well," I said.

"Do you like her?"

"She's all right."

After this there was another pause.

"At least there's Saturday," said Frizz.

"Yes!" I perked up at the thought of Saturday. We were all going to meet at Keri's place after lunch. We had agreed that we would meet up every weekend, taking it in turns to go to one another's houses.

"Will you come and pick me up?" said Frizz.

I promised that I would.

"Two o'clock," I said. "Be ready!"

I was so looking forward to Saturday! Seeing the others, telling all about our new schools. But there were still four whole days to go. It seemed like a lifetime!

Chapter 2

I dragged into school on Tuesday. I'd always loved school before, with Lily and Keri and Frizz. I'd wake up every morning thinking, "I wonder what will happen today!" And something always did happen! Sometimes it would be something funny like when Jessamy got locked in the lavatory and was there for simply hours. Or sometimes it would be something good, like me getting a gold star for a short story that I wrote, or Frizz having her art work pinned on the wall. Or maybe it would be something sad, like one of the hamsters dying, or something mysterious, like who scrawled rude words on the cloakroom wall, or something exciting, like a visitor coming to talk to us. But whatever it was, you just knew that you were part of it, because it was *your school*, where you belonged.

The High School wasn't my school! I didn't feel that I would ever belong! It was too grand; it was too big. All these girls had been together since Reception, and I was just an outsider. Well, me and a few others. But two of the others had come from the same school, and they were sticking together, and Jessamy had got her claws into Chloë and wasn't ever going to let go, and that just left me with limp old lettuce leaf.

Lettice was waiting for me outside the school gates. I was sort of half glad to see her, 'cos it is so horrid being on your own, and half irritated, like I wanted to snap at her to stop slithering round me all the time.

I could see her face bobbing about like a big pale moon. She was a very pale sort of person. She had very long pale hair and a very long pale nose and eyes that you couldn't have said, if anyone had asked you, what colour they were.

They weren't really any colour at all.

"Polly!" she squealed. She even had a pale sort of voice. "I got here early and I waited for you." She hooked her arm through mine, so that I was pinned next to her. "Tomorrow *you* can wait for *me*. That's only fair," she said. "Don't you think?"

"I suppose so," I said. I'd just caught sight of Chloë, on her own – that is, without Jessamy – and I *did* wish I could go and talk to her! But Lettice had me clamped really tight.

"We'll take it in turns," she said. "One day I'll wait, one day you can."

I watched as Chloë went walking across the playground. Actually, she didn't so much walk as bounce. She had this funny little thing that she did: step, spring, hop! Step, spring, hop!

"New girl," said Lettice. The way she'd said it, you'd think new girls were like something dogs do on pavements. Something you'd pick up in a poop scoop and chuck in the bin. I couldn't help wondering, in that case, why she kept slithering round me. I mean, she'd been with the others since Reception; why pick on a new girl?

If she'd tried to pick on Jessamy, Jessamy would just simply have ignored her. (Same as she was ignoring me.) Keri, if she had been there, would have just withered her with a glance. But Keri and Jessamy are both incredibly confident sort of people. They wouldn't ever be latched on to by someone like Lettice. I just didn't know how to get rid of her! I suppose it was, I was scared that if I did I would be on my own. There is nothing worse than being on your own.

So I obediently stayed by her side as we went to our classroom, and sat down next to her, and tried very hard not to notice that Chloë and Jessamy were giggling together over something Jessamy had in her desk.

I wondered how the others were doing. Lily, and Keri, and Frizz. Lily, most probably, would be doing ballet exercises. Bending and stretching and throwing her legs all about. Keri would be the centre of attention, 'cos Keri always is. I pictured her surrounded by a group of admiring girls. Frizz would be with Melanie Philpotts and Darcie White. That dreary pair! But even Melanie and Darcie had to be better than old wet lettuce leaf.

Mrs Pollard, our class teacher, came in. She said, "Good morning, girls!" and we all stood up and chorused, "Good morning, Mrs Pollard." Craig had hooted when I told Mum we had to do this. Mum approved of it, she said it was teaching us good manners; but I didn't think I was going to tell the others about it! They would only make fun of me.

At break time I walked round the playground with Lettice. Jessamy and Chloë were there kicking a football with another group from our class.

"Oh, look!" I said hopefully. "They're playing football!" I am not terribly sporty, in fact I am not really sporty at all, but I thought that even playing football would be better than being stuck on my own with Lettice.

I said, "Shall we go and join in?"

Lettice wouldn't. She yanked me off in the opposite direction. "We don't want to be bothered with them," she said. "We're a twosome!"

I didn't quite like to go barging in on my own, especially as I am not sporty. So I obediently stayed with Lettice and tried not to feel resentful.

"Who did you go round with last term?" I said.

She said, "Beverley Biddulph, but she started telling lies about me. And before her it was Katie Saunders, until she got mean. It was that Chantal that did it. She turned her against me. I hate her!"

These were three girls that were in our year. Chantal was really popular. She was the most popular girl in the whole class. She and Katie went round together, with Beverley just sort of tagging along.

"Chantal's always doing it," said Lettice. "She steals people."

Like Jessamy, I thought; and I wondered if Chantal was really as horrible as Lettice said she was or whether Lettice was just making it up. I wasn't making it up about Jessamy!

First class after break was French, when we were all divided into different sets. I was with Chloë and Katie and a few others from our class, plus people from Nightingale and Ashcroft. (We were Brontë, after the famous writer Charlotte Brontë, that wrote *Jane Eyre*. One of my favourite books! I was really glad I was in Brontë. I thought perhaps it was an omen and meant that one day I would also be a famous writer. Mum says I might be!)

All the people in our French group were the ones they thought might turn out to be good at languages. Like, all the people in my Maths group were the ones they knew were goofy at Maths! I am *extremely* goofy at Maths.

At the time I didn't realise I was in the top French set. I just thought it was chance that had thrown me and Chloë together. No Jessamy, no Lettice! Hooray!

I still didn't want to know whether Chloë would sit next to me, or anything. She might prefer to sit next to Katie. I mean, Katie was best friends with Chantal. And she was *popular*.

I should say that Katie is little and red-haired with freckles and that Chantal is black and just so-o-o-o beautiful it almost hurts. I would like to be beautiful but in fact I am quite ordinary. Brownish shortish hair, round face, round eyes, round cheeks. Glasses. I do have nice teeth! But teeth, alas, don't make a person beautiful.

Chloë's teeth stick out. And nobody could call her pretty, I don't think. But she is quaint and funny and makes people laugh.

"Hey, Polly!" She waved a hand. "Come and sit next to me!"

I didn't run as it's not allowed and they get cross if you break the rules, but I sort of bustled over to her, pushing people out of my way. Katie said, "Well, pardon *me*", and a girl from Nightingale asked me who I thought I was shoving, but I got to the empty desk and plonked myself next to Chloë.

"I've been dying to talk to you!" she said. "But you're always with your friend."

I was about to explain that Lettice wasn't really my friend, she was just someone who'd latched on to me, only Mrs Barker, the French teacher, was already in the room and calling for silence, and honestly they are just so strict at the High School, it's as much as your life's worth to even mouth something once a teacher's there.

That very first morning we learnt how to speak French! We learnt *Comment allez-vous?* meaning, How are you? And we learnt *Comment appellez-vous?* meaning, What is your name? We also learnt: *bonjour, bonsoir, petit déjeuner* and *merci beaucoup*. Ms Barker then told us to find partners and practise speaking to each other. So Chloë and me became partners, and Chloë made me laugh by saying all sorts of silly things. Like instead of *Comment appellez-vous?* she said *Comment APPLE-Y vous?* which just at first I didn't understand, so she had to explain it to me: "*Appellez...apple-y!* Munch munch munch!" And then I got it, and we both started saying silly things.

"*Comment...PEACHY-vous?*"

"*Comment...PLUMMY-vous?*"

I know it was silly but it was kind of fun. Probably because I was doing it with Chloë!

Next lesson was Gym, and all through it Chloë and me kept rushing up to each other going, "*Comment...MELONY-vous!*" and "*Comment... CURRANTY-vous!*" and dissolving into giggles.

We had to divide into three groups for Gym, according to height, which meant that me and Chloë were in the same one. (The shortest!) Lettice was in the middle lot, and Jessamy with the great tall ones. I could tell that she was really miffed at me being with Chloë, but there was nothing she could do about it. She kept giving us these sour looks, especially when we were giggling.

"What's so funny?" she hissed, as she swung towards us on the end of a rope.

"*Comment grapey-vous?*" said Chloë, and we both bent over and clutched our middles.

I could see that Jessamy was getting miffeder and miffeder. As we left the gym at the end of class she came rushing up and pushed herself rudely between us. "What were you two up to?" she said.

"Speaking French," giggled Chloë. "*Comment orangey-vous?*"

"French!" Jessamy tossed her head. "I know French! *Merci beaucoup*…that means *thank you.*"

Chloë said, "*Merci beaucoup*, have a cup of cocoa!" which set us off giggling all over again.

"Pathetic!" said Jessamy. But she was just jealous 'cos she couldn't join in. Ha ha!

After Gym it was break time, and I waited with a

sort of dread for Lettice to come and hook herself on to me. I wondered what would happen if I simply went off with Chloë. If I changed back into my ordinary clothes ever so fast and snatched up my bag and…

Too late! She was already heading for me.

"Polly!"

My heart went *clunk*, down into my shoes.

"I have to go, now, and see about my music lessons," said Lettice.

"Really? Oh, bother!" I said, brightening.

"Wait for me," she said. "I won't be long."

"Wait where?" I said.

"Outside. By the netball courts."

I waited for a few minutes, but then Chloë came over and said, "Come and make up a side!" and dragged me off to play basketball at the far end of the playground with Chantal and Katie and the others. I am not very good at basketball as I keep missing the ball (I think it's 'cos of wearing glasses) but Chloë wasn't much good either. She kept dashing around and leaping up and down and shouting, "Me, me!", but really she was too excitable. Jessamy and Chantal were the best.

It wasn't until the bell rang for the start of classes

that I remembered about Lettice. She came into the classroom all tight-lipped, not looking at me, and when I tried to say that I was sorry she simply dived under her desk lid and refused to speak. But I wasn't bothered as Chloë had whispered to me that she was going to see if a girl called Anna Wong would change desks so's I could sit with her and Jessamy at the back. Lettice could sulk if she wanted. See if I cared!

She very pointedly ignored me for the whole of the morning. It was quite restful, as a matter of fact. Then after lunch we had Maths, when I was in the goofy set. So, unfortunately, was Lettice. I'd hoped she'd go on ignoring me, but all of a sudden, for some reason, she decided to start talking again.

"I wouldn't want you to think I bear grudges," she said. "If you're really sorry, I'll forgive you."

"I just forgot," I said. "I was playing basketball with Chloë and the others."

"You don't want to mix with that crowd," said Lettice.

I said, "Why not? What's wrong with them?"

"They steal people," said Lettice. "People's friends... They steal them off them. And they tell lies! Chantal and Katie... They're always doing it."

She kept on and on, all through Maths. Every time

Mrs Burkett turned to write something on the board, Lettice leaned across and hissed things at me. "They're horrible! You can't trust them! You'll be sorry!"

I refused to budge. I wasn't yet sure how I felt about Chantal and Katie but I really didn't like Lettice very much. On the other hand, I didn't want to hurt her feelings, so I told her how me and Chloë had had our interviews together and how it had made a bond between us.

Lettice said crossly, "They've already told you lies about me, haven't they?" Nothing would convince her that they hadn't.

I asked Beverley about it during the afternoon break and she said that Lettice always thought people were saying things about her, or making up stories. "She's quarrelled with everybody, practically."

I thought that was really sad, but it didn't make me want to be friends with her, and by the end of the day she'd changed desks with Sonya Tingay and was sitting next to this very quiet girl called Susha. "I don't want to be friends with you any more," she said. So that was all right! At least I didn't have to waste time feeling sorry for her. I did feel a bit sorry for poor Susha. I imagined her being bullied and bossed and told what to do, but mainly I was just glad it wasn't me!

I went home at the end of Tuesday feeling a lot happier than I had at the end of Monday. A *whole* lot happier. I still missed Frizz and the others, of course. There were moments when I missed them quite horribly. I missed all our giggling and our gossip and the cosiness of belonging to the Gang of Four. But I'd done a bit of giggling with Chloë and I'd joined in the basketball game and I'd got rid of Lettice, hurray hurrah! So maybe the High School might not turn out to be quite so bad after all.

I got home and kissed Bundle and gave him a bit of a play with his ball, and Mum obviously saw that I was feeling happier 'cos she laughed and said, "Things are going better, I take it?"

"Better than they were," I said.

"Well, I knew they would," said Mum.

We were in the middle of tea when the telephone rang. Mum went to answer it.

"It's for you," she said. "It's Dawn."

She meant Frizz. Mum is so funny! She always calls her Dawn. It is her name, of course. Dawn Frizzell (pronounced Friz*elle*, as she is forever telling us). But we have called her Frizz for just about as long as I can remember.

I grabbed a piece of cake and rushed down the hall

to the telephone. "Frizz?" I said.

In reply she heaved this deep quivering sigh and said, "Polly?"

Chirpily, 'cos she sounded like she was in one of her glooms, I said, "*Comment allez-vous?*"

Frizz said, "What?"

"*How are you?*" I said. "Haven't you started French yet?"

Frizz said yes; but she didn't sound at all enthusiastic. In fact she sounded decidedly waterlogged. I did so hope she wasn't crying! Just as I was starting to feel happy.

"What's the matter?" I said.

It came bursting out at me, down the telephone. "I hate Heathfield!"

I pulled a face at myself in the mirror.

"Yesterday," I reminded Frizz, "you said it was OK."

"That was yesterday," mumbled Frizz.

"So what's changed?"

What had changed was Melanie and Darcie. They'd suddenly turned against Frizz and decided they didn't want her to be part of their gang.

"What gang?" I said. "How can they be a gang if there are only two of them?"

Frizz said there weren't only two. "They've got all

matey with these other girls."

I didn't know what to say. I knew how horrid it was when people turned against you. "Maybe tomorrow they'll change their minds," I said.

"They won't," said Frizz. "And anyway, I don't want to be part of their rotten gang. They're *pond* life."

"Total twonks," I said, bracingly.

I could understand how Frizz was feeling 'cos only yesterday I'd felt the same way. Now today I was feeling heaps happier and poor old Frizz was down in the dumps! I tried to think how I could cheer her up.

"Hold on till Saturday," I said.

"Saturday's days away," moaned Frizz.

"No, it's not," I said. "Only three! I'll come and pick you up and we'll go round to Keri's and it'll be just like it's always been. You'll see!"

I knew that it wouldn't be, really; I knew it couldn't be. Not with all of us at different schools. But Frizz is my bestest, bestest friend and I hated the thought of her being miserable.

"Three days," I said. "They'll go in a flash!"

Chapter 3

The days passed really quickly, just as I'd promised Frizz they would. It was the weekend almost before I knew it! I was really excited at the thought of meeting up with all the others. Frizz especially, 'cos she's my *oldest* friend, but Frizz and me had at least spoken on the phone. I was longing to hear how Lily and Keri were getting on!

Saturday afternoon, Mum drove me to Bridge Street, which is where Frizz lives with her mum and dad above their newsagent's shop. Frizz was ready and waiting. She was just as excited as I was! It seemed ages since we'd seen each other, though in fact it was only just over a week.

For some stupid reason I expected her to look different. Like, more grown-up or something. I mean, I'm not cool like Keri, always wearing the latest gear, but I had tried to look a little bit funky. This was our very first get-together since starting at new schools! So I'd put on my denim skirt and my new tie-dye top and sparkly tights and my trainers (not, alas, from Go Girl, but still quite cool).

Frizz was wearing these baggy old jeans and a plaid shirt that I just knew she'd had for years and that made her look really frumpy. Frizz has absolutely no sense of style! She is what Mum calls "homely" but she could look ever so much prettier if she just made a bit of an effort. I mean, I know her mum and dad aren't rich, but neither are mine or Lily's. Lily has this advantage, that she is so cute and so tiny that she would look great in practically anything. She would look great in a bin bag! But what I'm saying is you don't have to spend a fortune.

Well, anyway, I didn't say anything to Frizz 'cos she's ever so easily upset and I didn't really mind what she looked like. I was just so glad to see her! And to be honest, after the first five minutes

I just forgot all about it.

Keri's house is in The Glades and is really posh. Keri has her own private sitting room, which her dad had put in specially for her at the top of the house. It's brilliant! It even has a balcony, where we all lie out in summer, getting a tan. (Using loads of sun block, natch!)

Mum dropped us off and said that she would be back at six o'clock to collect us. Me and Frizz followed Keri up the stairs. I was really glad that I had got a bit dressed up as Keri was looking dead groovy. As usual! She's very tall and slim, with masses of gorgeous red hair, which she'd scooped up into a ponytail and fixed with glittery tinsel hair clips. She was wearing a blue vest top and designer jeans and lots of sparkly bangles.

Lily turned up a few minutes later. She came bounding up the stairs with a big grin on her face. "Howdy, folks!"

"*Lily!*" we shrieked.

She was dressed all butch in a Levi jacket, short skirt and boots. And *still* looked cute! On her head she had this really great cowboy hat, which naturally we all wanted to try on.

"Man," said Keri. "I have got to get one of these!"

"Let me, let me!" begged Frizz.

But it didn't suit Frizz the way it suited Lily. Instead of perking her up and making her look all bright and cheeky, it made her look like a pudding. I could tell she was disappointed. It's like when I go into shops and try things on and always secretly hope they'll make me look like Britney Spears, or someone, and they never do. I gaze in the mirror and I'm still just *me*. Little and round and ordinary. So I knew how Frizz was feeling. She took off the hat and said, "I hate hats, anyway."

"Some people can wear them and some people can't," said Keri. "It's just one of those things." Then she looked at Frizz and went, "Oh, *honestly*. We have got to do something about your hair!" She grabbed hold of Frizz and sat her down, with a plonk, in front of the dressing table. "Just stay still. Don't move!"

Me and Lily sat watching as Keri picked up a brush and beat and tweaked and twizzled, piling Frizz's rather limp brown hair on top of her head and finally fixing it with one of her own glittery tinsel clips.

"There!" she said. "That's much better!"

It was, I have to admit. Frizz stared timidly at herself in the mirror.

"It makes you look dead sophisticated!" I said.

Frizz's cheeks turned slowly pink.

"You can have the clip," said Keri. "I've got plenty of others."

Frizz's cheeks grew even pinker. It's funny, with Keri. There are times she can get quite impatient with poor old Frizz, like she tells her to get real or grow up; then other times she kind of takes her under her wing and makes sure she looks OK and wears the right clothes and gives her stuff, like skirts and tops and tights, that she says she doesn't need any more.

"Do my hair like that!" said Lily.

"No." Keri shook her head. "You've got the wrong sort of face. It wouldn't suit you."

"What about me?" I said.

"No. You two would just look silly. You're too small. You've got to be tall, like me and Frizz."

Oh! That was *such* a nice thing for Keri to say! You could almost see Frizz preening. It's times like that when I know why we've stayed friends for so long. I mean, Frizz is the one I'm closest to, and Lily is really sweet, the sort of person it is easy to love, but with Keri you sometimes think, "I can't stand that girl!" Like when she is being so-o-o superior, and making you feel like a dung beetle. And then next moment she can just be so kind, and so generous, that you feel like hugging her!

"Well, come on," urged Lily. She settled, cross-legged, on one of the big puffy floor cushions that Keri had scattered about. "Let's all tell what it's like!"

She meant being at new schools.

"OK. You first," said Keri.

"Well…" Lily rocked backwards and forwards. She scrunched her face up into this impish grin. "It's bliss being without Jessamy!"

"*Apart* from that,' I said.

Apart from that, said Lily, she was really enjoying herself. "Dancing classes *every day*!" She said that it was hard work and that the competition was really fierce. "Some of the others are so good I got a bit depressed, just at first."

"I bet they're not as good as you," said Frizz.

"They are," said Lily. "They're better. It's frightening! I'm going to have to put in *loads* of extra practice."

She turned down the corners of her mouth as she said it, but you could tell that she thought it was all worthwhile. It was what she really wanted to do.

Next, it was Keri's turn, and she told us about her boarding school, how she shared a dorm with three other girls whose names were Jemima, Joanna and Alice. Jemima had a pony which she kept at the school, so Keri was going to ask her mum and dad if she could have one, too.

"But you can't ride," I said.

"So I'll *learn*," said Keri.

Joanna's mum was an actress we'd all heard of 'cos she was in a TV soap, and Alice's dad was an MP that we probably ought to have heard of but hadn't, which Keri seemed to think was very ignorant of us. (Though I bet she'd never heard of him, either, before she went to boarding school!)

"It sounds like fun," said Lily.

"It's absolutely fabbo!"

"But aren't you glad you can come home at weekends?" said Frizz.

"Mm…" Keri thought about it. "I s'ppose so."

Frizz's forehead wrinkled into a frown. "You wouldn't want to be there *the whole term*?"

"Dunno. Might do. Except I wouldn't see you lot! It would be so great," said Keri, "if we could all be there!"

"I'd miss my mum and dad," wailed Frizz.

"I'd miss Bundle," I said. "And my mum and dad," I added, just to keep Frizz company. I mean, I *would* miss them, but I wouldn't have said so if it hadn't been for Frizz.

"Honestly, you are such a couple of babies!" jeered Keri.

"I wouldn't miss my brother," I said.

"No, well. *Brothers.*' And then she said this weird thing. She said, "It's just as well you've got one though, or you'd have no experience."

"Of what?" I said.

"Boys!" said Lily, and gave a cackling screech of laughter and rolled backwards off her cushion. "You're the only one that doesn't have any!"

At the High School is what she meant. I pulled a face. Who'd *want* any? Not me!

"So, come on, then," said Keri, "tell! What's it like, the boffin place?"

I said, "It's not a boffin place. It's just they make you work really really hard."

"But do you *like* it?"

I said that it was OK, though we had positively stacks of homework.

"And Jessamy is there!" Lily gave another cackle of laughter and rolled back on to her cushion. "Ooh, groo! Jessamy Jones!"

"I hope you don't have anything to do with her?" said Keri.

"Not if I can help it," I said.

We talked about the High School for a bit and I agreed with Keri that the uniform is total grot (I am such a coward!) then Lily asked Frizz how she was getting on at Heathfield.

In a small, tight voice Frizz said, "It's all right."

"Well, it ought to be,' said Keri. "I mean, it's not like you're on your own."

"It's not like you've got Jessamy!" Lily gave a chortle and upended herself so that her legs went right back over her head and touched the floor behind her.

"And at least you don't have to wear that yucky High School uniform," said Keri.

At this point, Keri's mum called up the stairs that she'd got some tea ready if we'd like to come down, so we didn't talk any more about Heathfield. Which was probably just as well.

At six o'clock Mum arrived to pick up me and Frizz, and we all arranged to meet at the same time next week at Frizz's place.

"It's been so brilliant!" said Keri. "I've really been longing to meet up with you guys!"

"Me too," said Lily, and she flung herself first at me, and then at Frizz, and kissed us. Frizz went all pink, but I could see that she was pleased.

"Well! It looks like you've all had a good time," said Mum, as we drove off.

"Yes! We have," said Frizz. "Oh, I *wish* we could all be together again! It just seems right when we're together."

I knew what she meant. It was like living in two different worlds. The *new* world, of school-without-the-others; and the *old* world, just as it used to be.

"It'll work itself out," said Mum. "You'll see!"

I could tell that Frizz didn't believe her, and I wasn't sure that I did, either. But at least we had our weekends to look forward to!

Chapter 4

At school I went round all the time now with Jessamy and Chloë. We were sort of unofficially part of Chantal's gang. Well, Jessamy was part of it; me and Chloë sometimes were and sometimes weren't. But we didn't tag on, like Beverley. We had more pride! If we weren't invited we went off and did our own thing.

We had lots of fun, me and Chloë! Like in English Mrs Barber said that our class project for this term was to produce our own magazine. We all had to contribute. Some people were going to write articles, like on fashion, or beauty, or hairstyles. Others were gong to do quizzes, or letters, or reviews. We were even going to have photographs.

We all got to choose, so me and Chloë chose the problem page. We were going to call it, SHARE YOUR PROBS WITH CLO AND POL. So when we weren't joining in with Chantal and the others, we were sitting on a bench, with notebooks and pencils, giggling over imaginary problems.

Dear Clo and Pol,
Please help! I am only twelve years old and already I take a size 52 shoe. I keep tripping over my own feet! It is so embarrassing. What can I do? – Marlene

Dear Marlene,
Be brave! There is only one solution: ask your dad if you can borrow his saw. Best of luck!

Dear Clo and Pol,
I am a vegetarian who doesn't like vegetables! What can I eat? I am growing desperate!!! – Faydee

Dear Faydee,
Stop this nonsense immediately. Eat fruit!

People kept coming up to us and asking what we were giggling about, but we wouldn't tell them! I did tell Frizz when she rang up. I mean, she didn't ask me what I was giggling about 'cos obviously I wasn't giggling at that particular time; but when she asked me how things were (which she did a lot) I said, "We're doing this magazine and I'm doing the problem page. I'm doing it with this girl, Chloë, that was at my interview," and I read out our latest one.

Dear Clo and Pol,
My best friend Lizzie won't hang out with me any more. She says my eyes are too close together! I don't know what to do as we have been best friends for simply ages and I really miss her. Can you suggest anything? – Ida Ho.

Dear Ida,
Have you thought of buying an eye patch? You can get some really funky ones! And if you only have one eye, your friend can hardly complain that it is too close, can she? Give it a go!

Well, I thought it was funny. All Frizz said was, "That would be horrid, if someone's best friend behaved like that."

"It's only made up," I said.

"I know," said Frizz. "But it would still be horrid."

"Frizz, it's just a *joke*," I said.

"Why are you doing jokey ones?" said Frizz. "Why not do real ones?"

"Well, because..." I didn't really know! It had never occurred to us. I said lamely that we'd thought jokey ones would be more fun.

Frizz said, "Oh."

She was very down. I knew she wasn't happy at Heathfield without me and the others. Melanie and Darcie still wouldn't let her be part of their gang, and everybody else, she said, had already paired off. I couldn't understand why Melanie and Darcie were being so mean, but Frizz said it was because they'd once tried to join our gang at Juniors and Keri had told them to shove off.

"She's just upset so many people," said Frizz.

It is true that Keri can be rather outspoken, but it seemed unfair that poor Frizz was having to pay the price. Frizz never hurt anyone! She is a very kind and gentle person. Sometimes when I was with Chloë I would come over all guilty and think that I oughtn't to be giggling and happy when my best and oldest friend was so utterly miserable.

"Well, anyway," I said, hoping to cheer her up, "I'll see you on Saturday. We'll have fun!"

We always have fun at Frizzle's. It's fun right from the very start, when you go in through this little secret door at the side of the shop, *squeeze* along a narrow passage and make your way up three flights of twisty turny stairs until you get to the attic, which is where Frizz has her bedroom. It is the sweetest little room imaginable!

Even though Keri's is the poshest, and the biggest, and Lily's is the most interesting, and mine is mine and just how I like it, Frizzle's is my most *most* favourite. It is so dinky! Like a room in a doll's house.

We all love Frizz's place; even Keri, who you might think would sneer at it. But she doesn't! I was ever so looking forward to going there. And then on Thursday Jessamy announced that she was inviting people back to her place for tea.

"Saturday," she said. "But only *special* people. Only you two" – that was me and Chloë. Me! That at the beginning she wouldn't even talk to! "And Chantal and Katie. Not anybody else."

"Not Beverley?" said Chloë.

"No." Jessamy frowned. "She's not really one of us."

Beverley wasn't – but I was! For a little while I was all cock-a-hoop, 'cos although I really didn't like Jessamy I did like the idea of belonging. And then I asked her what time we had to be there, and she said, "Early! Two o'clock. Then we can do things and have fun."

My face must have fallen, 'cos Chloë, rather anxiously, said, "What's the matter? Can't you come?"

"I've already arranged to do something else!" I wailed.

"Well, suit yourself," said Jessamy. "I'll ask Beverley, if you'd rather."

"No, don't!" begged Chloë. She looked at me, beseechingly. "Couldn't you get out of it?"

I didn't really see how I could. But I was ever so tempted! Chloë kept on at me all day. "Oh Polly, do come! Otherwise it'll be Jessamy sucking up to Katie and Chantal the whole time and I'll be stuck with Beverley!"

"Beverley's all right," I said. I mean, I had to be fair. "She's quite nice."

"Yes," said Chloë, "but I can't giggle with her like I can with you!"

In the end I promised that I would think about it

and let her know. Jessamy said, "You'd better make up your mind by tomorrow."

"I will," I said. "I will!"

I wrestled with my conscience all the way home and all through tea. Mum noticed. She said, "Pollee... is anybody there? You're looking all far-away and mumpish!"

I sighed and said, "Why is it that you can spend *days* waiting for something nice to happen, and then two nice things go and happen at the same time and you have to miss out on one of them?"

Craig said, "That's life, kiddo!"

He's always saying things like that, trying to sound cool and grown-up. In fact, he just sounds stupid.

"If it's life," I said, "then life's not fair!"

"Who said it was?" said Craig.

"What's the problem?" Mum pushed the biscuit tin towards me. Absently, I helped myself to one. (It turned out to be ginger, which I *hate*.) "What nice things are happening at the same time?"

I said, "One is meeting Lily and Keri at Frizz's on Saturday, and the other is going to tea with Jessamy. *Also* on Saturday!"

"I thought Jessamy was the one you didn't like?" said Mum. She'd had to sit through hours of me going on about Jessamy.

"I don't, specially," I said, "but Chloë's going to be there!"

"Well, I really can't help you," said Mum. "These things happen. I'm afraid it's something you'll have to work out for yourself."

I spent the next hour dithering. First I decided one thing, then I decided another. I'd just *positively* decided that I would tell Frizz I couldn't make it – I mean, I'd seen her last week and I'd be seeing her next week – when the telephone rang and guess what? It was Frizz. All in a twitter about Saturday.

"I'm going to make a cake!"

"Make a cake?" I said.

"Yes! We have cookery tomorrow morning, and we're going to make cakes! I'm going to do a chocolate one with chocolate icing. Lashings of it! Inside, as well." She giggled. She sounded really turned on by the thought of making a cake. "It's going to be sickly as sickly!"

"Lily won't eat any," I said. "You know what she's like."

"Oh, well, Lily! If she wants to go round like a stick insect," said Frizz, "that's up to her. You and me and Keri will eat it all!"

What could I do? I couldn't suddenly break it to her that I wasn't going. Instead, I had to break it to Chloë next morning, and then I had to tell Jessamy, who tossed her head and said, "That's it, then! I'll ask Beverley."

In a way, it was just as well Frizz rang when she did 'cos if I hadn't gone she would have been on her own with Keri. Lily didn't show up!

"She can't make it," said Keri. "She's got this special class, with somebody from the Royal Ballet. She's dead excited about it!"

"That's all right," I said, "She wouldn't have eaten any cake anyway."

"We can pig the lot!" giggled Frizz.

But then Keri announced that *she* couldn't eat any, either, 'cos she was going on a diet. "I'm getting too fat," she said.

She didn't look fat to me. I was the one that was getting fat if anyone was! I mean, I am just naturally rather round. Stubby, Mum says. But somebody had to eat Frizz's cake. Frizz was so proud of it! And it was a really good one, too, I have to admit. I had three slices!

"That is just so gross," said Keri.

"Yum yum," said Frizz, rubbing her tummy.

"Yes, yum yum," I said, 'cos I have to be loyal to Frizz.

Keri's mum came quite early to pick her up, so for a while me and Frizz were on our own.

"Wouldn't it be lovely," said Frizz, licking her fingers and dabbing at cake crumbs, "if you could transfer to Heathfield?"

"What, from the High School?" I said.

"People do," said Frizz. "Like if the work's too much for them. If they can't hack it."

What did she mean, if they couldn't hack it? I hoped she wasn't talking about me! I'd got an A+ for my last essay for Mrs Barber, and I could almost hold a conversation in French. I could say, *Je m'appelle Polly* and *J'ai onze ans* and *Quelle heure est-il?* And *Bonjour, comment allez-vous?* I could hack it!

"There's this girl in our class," said Frizz, "Jonquil. Her sister transferred. Her mum and dad decided the pressure was too much for her. They said the High School is just a forcing house. It pushes people too hard."

"I don't feel pushed," I said. "I know we have masses of homework, but—"

"Well, this is it," said Frizz. "They're pushing you.

58

It's what they do. Like a sausage machine, just putting people in for exams."

She'd obviously heard someone say it; it wasn't the sort of thing she would have thought of for herself. Probably this Jonquil.

"Actually," I said, "I *like* it at the High School. I wouldn't *want* to transfer. I *like* having lots of homework."

"Oh, well. Y-yes. Of course! I only meant – I mean – I didn't mean..."

Frizz burbled into silence. It is ever so easy to frighten her. But she shouldn't have said that about me not hacking it!

"I just thought it would be fun if we were together," she mumbled.

So then of course I felt mean and had to say that I thought it would be fun, too. Which I did. Except that I couldn't somehow see Frizz and Chloë getting on together, and I quite liked the idea of having one friend for school and one for out of school.

Frizz sighed and said, "You're becoming ever such a boffin."

"I'm not!" I said. "But if I am, I don't mean to."

"You can't help it," said Frizz, sadly. "It's just the way you're made."

When I got home I rang Chloë to ask her how the tea party had gone. She said, "Oh, you should have been there! It was really funny! Jessamy practically *crawled*, on her hands and knees…'*Oh, Chantal,*'" – she put on this oozing, yucky, horribly humble sort of voice – "'*you are so PRETTY, you are so CLEVER, you are so WONDERFUL… Oh, Chantal, let me kiss your feet!*'"

"Nauseating," I said.

"You are telling me," said Chloë. "I spent the whole time playing with the dog. She has ever such a lovely dog! He's called Benjy and he's just so beautiful!"

I hadn't realised that Chloë was a dog person. I was glad about that. It meant that when I invited her round, she wouldn't be scared of Bundle! But hearing about Benjy made me all the more miffed that I hadn't been there. I'd made this *huge* personal sacrifice, just for Frizz, and then she'd had the nerve to suggest I might want to to transfer from the High School in case I couldn't hack it! What cheek! I knew she hadn't meant to insult me but it had really hurt my pride, her saying that. Sometimes I think Frizz doesn't quite realise.

"Let's you and me make a date for you coming

round here," I said to Chloë.

"On a Saturday," said Chloë.

"Sunday would be best," I said. Saturdays were for the Gang of Four. We'd made it Saturday 'cos of Keri having to go back to school on Sunday afternoons. "Would a Sunday be OK?" I said.

Chloë said that it would, and we agreed that we would ask our mums. And that it would just be the two of us.

"Not Jessamy!"

We chanted it together, and giggled.

Chapter 5

A few days later, I got to school to find an envelope on my desk. A pink one, with crinkly edges and my name written in gold and a little furry sticker in the shape of a raspberry in one corner. Really sweet!

I opened it, wonderingly. Inside was an invitation to a party. Katie Saunders!!! I couldn't believe it! Me – invited to Katie Saunders' party! Katie was almost as popular as Chantal, while I was just, like, nobody.

Chloë had got one, too. But not everybody had! Only six people from our year. Me and Chloë, Jessamy, Beverley, Chantal of course, and a girl called Emily

Walsh from Nightingale that Katie had been friends with in Juniors.

I got home and told Mum about it and she laughed and said, "You make it sound like an invitation to take tea with the Queen!"

"Well, but Katie is *really* popular," I said.

"And we must get in with the right set, mustn't we?" said Mum.

I crinkled my nose. I had this distinct suspicion that Mum was teasing me, though I couldn't think why. Craig was there (unfortunately) and heard our conversation. He said, "You're a right creep, you are!" So I bashed him on the head with my school bag.

I was dying to tell the others about it! Keri never seemed to mind boasting about her new friends, the one with the pony and the one with the mum that was an actress, so I didn't see why I shouldn't do a bit of boasting of my own. I thought I would just toss it out sort of casually, like, "Hey, guess what? I've been invited to this party! A girl called Katie Saunders...she's one of the most popular people in the class."

Not boasting, just saying. But then as it happened I didn't even mention it. 'Cos everything went wrong and I forgot all about it.

We were supposed to be meeting at Lily's that

Saturday. But Friday evening Keri rang. "Meet at my place," she said. "Lily can't make it."

"Not again," I wailed.

"She just rang me. She's really sorry! She's going to tell Frizz. I said I'd tell you."

"So what is it this time?" I said.

"It's not her fault," said Keri. "It's this woman."

I said, "What woman?"

"This person from the Royal Ballet. She's giving more special classes."

"You'd think Lily would have enough classes," I said.

"Yes, I know," said Keri. "But this woman is special."

Keri had to stick up for Lily; I understood that. I mean, she and Lily are best friends, same as me and Frizz. You have to be loyal to your best friend. But I couldn't help thinking that Lily wasn't being very loyal to us. She'd had a special lesson last Saturday! Surely she didn't need another one? I knew she had to put her dancing first, but I did wish this Royal Ballet person could give her special classes at some other time! Things just weren't the same without Lily.

When we got there, Keri was in one of her super-cool moods, like this was Buckingham Palace and she was the Queen, giving a tea party. She gets like this every now and again. If Lily had been there, she would have laughed her out of it. I just took no notice. I mean, that's Keri. But it made poor old Frizz really nervous, so that she started breaking things and dropping things and knocking things over. Like she dropped a bag of crisps she was eating and then went and trampled on it so it all got ground into the carpet. Next she knocked a glass elephant off a shelf and it smashed against the edge of a table and its trunk fell off.

Keri said airily that it didn't matter. "I can always get another one."

Which of course made Frizz feel guilty, which made her even more nervous, so that she reached out for her drink and sprayed bright orange fizzy pop all down the wall.

"Don't worry about it," said Keri. "It'll sponge off."

We all knew that it wouldn't. Orange is almost the *worst*. Orange and cherry. You can't get them off no matter how hard you try. Frizz mopped at it despairingly with a paper towel.

"Look, just leave it," said Keri. "It really doesn't matter."

Poor old Frizzle just stood there, clutching her

paper towel (now bright orange). Silently, Keri held out the waste basket. I saw Frizzle's cheeks glow scarlet, and I just knew that if I didn't come to her rescue she was going to do something really disastrous, like stepping backwards onto a plate and crunching it, or maybe just bursting into tears. I had to act quickly!

"Are you learning French?" I said to Keri. "How far have you got? Have you done *merci beaucoup*?" I giggled. "*Merci beaucoup*, have a cup of cocoa!"

Frizz tittered, then hiccuped.

"And *Comment apple-y vous*?" I giggled again. Frizz hiccuped. "*Appley-vous, peachey-vous...*"

Frizz was now hiccuping fit to bust.

Desperately, I gabbled on. "*Comment CURRANTY-vous*? *Comment—*" Another giggle burst out of me. I was starting to sound like a hysterical parrot, but now that I'd started I couldn't seem to stop. "*Comment...*" I giggled again, and nearly choked myself. "*Comment GRAPEY-vous*? *Comment PLUMMY-vous*? *Comment...*"

My voice finally trailed away into silence. Keri was giving me one of those looks, like I was a ball of snot or something stinky in a corner. "It's what we say," I said, lamely.

"Who's we?" said Keri.

"Oh! Just this girl that's in my French class."

"C-Chloë." That was Frizz, between hiccups.

"And you go round talking like that?"

"It's just for fun," I said.

"Some fun," said Keri.

I hung my head. I supposed it was rather childish. But if Lily had been there she would have joined in! She would have jumped around, being a peach or a plum. She would have invented little dances and thought of new fruit. *Comment DATEY-vous? Comment STRAWBERRY-vous?*"

Without her it was just idiotic and stupid. It made me feel ashamed. For the first time ever, I felt almost relieved when it was time to go.

"Where do we meet next week?" said Frizz.

"It ought to be Lily's place," I said.

"I'll tell her," said Keri. "I'll make sure she's there!"

It's always kind of weird – though in a nice way! – when we meet at Lily's. Lily's bedroom isn't like a place for sleeping in. Everything's flat against the wall, with this big empty space in the middle for her to practise her dancing in.

When we go round she chucks pillows on the floor and we all sit around on the bed and the cushions while Lily flits about doing bendy things and stretchy things and things with her feet.

Lily is one of those people, she can never just sit still. A teacher at school once said, "Lily Stubbs, you are in constant motion!" It's true; she always has to be moving round. I sometimes wonder where she gets all her energy from. I mean, she is just so tiny.

So, anyway, the following Saturday there we were at Lily's, me and Frizz on our cushions, Lily waving her arms and legs in the air – and no Keri! She simply never showed. And didn't even bother to let us know!

"She was going to come," said Lily. "I talked to her on the phone and she said that she was."

"Never mind her," said Frizz. "You're here!"

Lily giggled. "Well, it's my place!"

I asked her if her special classes had finished and she said yes, they had. She said it almost regretfully, as if she would have liked them to continue. Every Saturday afternoon.

"It was brilliant!" She clasped her hands together in a way that would have looked just too naff for words if anyone else had done it, but Lily can do almost anything and get away with it. She twirled a little exultant twirl across her shiny bedroom floor.

"Natasha is my favouritest, *favouritest* dancer! If I could be like anyone, it would be like Natasha! Last week she danced some of the Sugar Plum Fairy for us... Miss Banks said we were really privileged. She said this was a moment to treasure, that we would always remember...and I will!" vowed Lily.

Me and Frizz listened in a kind of awed silence. We had never even heard of this Natasha person! By the end of the afternoon, however, we knew all there was to know about her. Plus we got to see Lily dancing the Sugar Plum Fairy for us – and Lily's mum never once yelled up the stairs to "Stop making that noise!" Maybe because Lily didn't really make any.

So we had a nice time, but things still didn't feel the same. We missed Keri just as much as we'd missed Lily. It's true she can be one great big enormous PAIN, but she is also a lot of fun. It's always Keri that organises us, and decides what we're going to do. Without her we were at a bit of a loss; I even missed her superior yawns and her spiky comments. We were the Gang of Four, and three on their own just didn't work.

After I'd got home, I rang Keri's number. It was her mum who answered the phone.

"Oh, hello, Polly!" she said. "Keri's not back yet. Do you want to leave a message?"

"I just wondered where she was?" I said.

"You mean she didn't call you?" Her mum sounded surprised. Also a bit annoyed. "She should have called you! I told her to. She suddenly got an invitation to go and spend the weekend with a girl from school. She was very excited because the girl has a pony and they were going to take the pony back with them and Keri was going to ride it. But that's no excuse for forgetting her manners!"

I didn't think it was, either; I thought it was very rude. She turned up the following week, at my place, and was totally high-handed about it. Well, I thought she was.

"Oh, yah, I'm sorry," she said. "It all happened in such a rush. And look, you guys! I'm afraid I won't be able to make next week either."

She didn't say *why* she wouldn't be able to make next week. I thought that was pretty high-handed, too, but I wasn't going to ask! I wouldn't give her the satisfaction. It was Frizz who said why not? Frizz quite often steps in when I won't.

Keri pulled a face. "I've got to go to this wedding. It's a dead bore. I'd much rather be here with you. But

I've got to go, it's my cousin, and I'm going to be a bridesmaid!"

What she meant was, she was just longing to get all dressed up and show off. I mean, you could tell.

"Oh, well, it doesn't really matter," said Frizz. "I expect we'll manage OK."

Keri looked at her suspiciously. Lily stifled a giggle. You can never be quite sure, with Frizz, whether she's saying these things in all innocence, or whether she's having a sly little dig. Like, in this case, sticking a pin into the great inflated bubble of Keri's self-importance.

"I can come the week after," said Keri. Suddenly, she was starting to sound a bit anxious. "I really hate not to be here. It's...it's my *cousin*.'

"Bring us some wedding cake," said Lily.

"Don't see the point of that," I said. "Considering you won't eat it!"

"No, 'cos I'm terrified of getting *fat*," said Lily. She sucked in her stomach, which practically touches her backbone to begin with. "Natasha is so slim! Someone said that when she's on stage she looks like a wisp of smoke."

"Obviously anorexic," said Keri. "Personally I've given up on the idea of dieting. I've decided it's better to be healthy."

Lily instantly objected that she *was* healthy. She said that for ballet you couldn't afford to be "all lumpy". Keri said, "If by that you mean having a figure—" at which we embarked on a long and heated discussion about fatness and thin-ness and bodies in general, which is the kind of thing that happens when Keri is with us. I have to admit that she is quite a stimulating sort of person, even if you do sometimes want to throw her to the ground and jump on her.

"Next week at my place," said Frizz, as we left.

"Have a good time," said Keri. "I'll think of you!"

In the car on the way home Frizz said, "We can do without her, if she doesn't want to come."

"Well, but I suppose if it's her cousin's wedding," I said.

I wasn't making excuses for her, but weddings are things you can't always get out of, especially if you're a bridesmaid. On the other hand, you don't have to keep having special classes on a Saturday. I wouldn't have thought so. I would have thought classes five days a week were enough for anyone. But on Tuesday evening Lily rang me up. She sounded really apologetic.

"Oh, Polly, we've got another class!"

I said, "Not Natasha again?"

"No! It's not ballet this time, it's jazz."

"But I thought you wanted to do ballet and be like Natasha?" I said.

"I do," said Lily. "But you can't always tell. I mean, suppose I grow too tall, or the wrong shape, or something? Oh, Polly, I'm sorry!"

"Have you told Frizz?" I said.

Lily said no, she was hoping that I would. I knew why she was leaving it to me: it was because we were meeting at Frizz's place and she felt guilty.

"Well, I *will* tell her," I said. "But it ought to be you doing it, really!"

"But you're her best friend," pleaded Lily. Like it was the duty of people's best friends to break bad news to them.

"I'm only doing it just this once," I said.

"It'll only be just this once," said Lily.

I said, "Huh!" and put the receiver back and dialled Frizz's number. I thought I'd better get it over with right away 'cos I reckoned she was going to be really upset. Which she was, though not as much as I'd expected.

"I knew this would happen," she said. "I knew it would all start to break up!"

"It's only just this one time," I said.

"You'll still be coming, won't you?" said Frizz.

I assured her that I would and she cheered up immediately.

"That's all right, then! It'll just be the two of us. We'll have fun! We've got Home Ec. on Friday, we're doing puddings. I'll make a pudding just for you and me! I'm going to do a really gooey one...nuts and fudge and *chocolate*." She giggled. "We'll put on simply kilos!"

I was a bit alarmed by this as I wasn't sure that I wanted to put on kilos. I mean, I wouldn't want to look like a wisp of smoke, but who wants to roll about like a beach ball?

I suggested to Frizz that perhaps it would be better if she made a plainer sort of pudding, like rhubarb crumble or something, but she said scornfully that anyone could make rhubarb crumble.

"I want to do something special! And if Lily's not going to be there it won't matter if it's fattening."

I thought glumly that I had better starve myself for the next few days, but of course when it came to it I couldn't resist eating French fries at lunch time and a chocolate bar during break. Bounce, bounce, bounce!

Friday morning I had a horrible shock. Katie came

up to us, to me and Chloë, and hissed, "Don't forget! Tomorrow."

I said, "Tomorrow?" And then I remembered... It was her party! Katie's party! And I was supposed to be going to see Frizz!

Woe. I arrived home with my face all drear and drooping. Mum took one look and went, "Uh oh! Something's happened. What is it? You'd better tell me!'

"I don't know what to do!" I wailed.

"About what?" said Mum.

So I told her about the party, and about Lily and Keri not being able to turn up at our meeting, and how Frizz was looking forward to it just being me and her. "She's making us a pudding!"

"Oh, dear," said Mum. "You really are getting in a muddle with your social engagements, aren't you?"

I nodded, miserably.

"This," said Mum, "is why people keep diaries. They write things down. Then they don't get into this sort of mess."

"I will," I said, "in future. But *what am I going to do now?*"

I sort of roared this last bit. Mum shook her head.

"Polly, I told you before... I can't help you."

"But you've got to!" I bellowed.

Mum looked at me. "Just how important is this party?"

"It's very important!"

"I don't quite see how it can be *very* important," said Mum, "considering you'd forgotten all about it."

"It is!" I screamed. "It's Katie Saunders's!"

"Is she someone you really like?"

"Yes! Well – yes. I do quite like her."

"As much as you like Dawn?"

That was a mean question. Mum knows that Frizz is my best friend.

"This is a *party*," I said. "And I said that I'd go! I accepted the invitation...in *writing!*"

"So you want to go to the party," said Mum. "So go!"

"But what about Frizz?"

"What about her?"

"She'll be upset!"

"That bothers you?"

I looked at Mum, reproachfully.

"She'll feel I've deserted her!"

"So go round to her place..."

"But..."

"But what?" said Mum.

76

"That's what I did last time! I had to miss out!"

"In that case," said Mum, "I'm surprised you've been foolish enough to let it happen again."

Really, there are times when Mum is no help at all. At six o'clock, when Dad came in, she said, "Polly, have you decided what you're doing about tomorrow?"

"Not yet," I muttered. "I'm still thinking."

First I would think one thing – I can't let Frizz down! Then I would think another – I can't not go to the party! Then I would get cross and think, bother Frizz! Bother and blast! I *will* go to the party. Then I would at once feel mean and think, but she'll be so upset! She'll be by herself!

I was still thinking one thing and then another when the telephone rang and it was Chloë. She was all of a dither about what she was going to wear to the party. She wanted me to advise her. She said, "What are you going to wear?"

We had this long and earnest discussion, and by the end of it I had made up my mind: I was going to the party! I'd already made one sacrifice for Frizz; I didn't see why I should have to make another.

Ever so quickly, before I could have second

thoughts, I snatched up the receiver and punched out Frizz's number.

"Polly!" She squealed at me down the telephone. "I've made it! A lovely big gooey pudding!"

My heart went *clunk*. "Will it keep?" I said.

"Keep? Till tomorrow? Yes!"

"No, I mean..." I swallowed. "The thing is," I said, "I've just realised...I can't make it tomorrow! I've got something else...a school thing. It's really boring. I'd forgotten all about it!"

From the other end of the phone came this really *loud* silence.

"Frizz?" I said. "I'm sorry! Honestly! I was really looking forward to it." More of the loud silence; then in a small voice Frizz said, "What about Sunday? It would keep till Sunday."

Panic set in. I couldn't go on Sunday! I'd asked Chloë to come round. I'd asked her ages ago!

Desperately I said, "I can't! It'll have to be next Saturday."

"It won't keep till then," said Frizz.

"Not even in the fridge?"

"No! It has to be eaten straight away."

"You could always make another one," I said. "One for next week. Then we'd all be there!"

Frizz said she couldn't make another one; they weren't doing puddings any more. "It's vegetables next week."

"Oh, Frizz," I said, "I'm sorry!"

"Doesn't matter," said Frizz.

But I knew that it did; I knew that she was trying not to cry.

"It isn't fair!" I thought, as I put down the phone. I'd made new friends; why couldn't Frizz? It didn't mean that she wasn't my *best* friend any more, just that now I had other friends, as well. Why couldn't she just get a life???

I hadn't wanted to eat her horrible sicky pudding anyway.

Chapter 6

It was a rotten party. A *rotten* one.

The day began so well! First thing after breakfast I went into town with Mum to buy a present for Katie and get myself a new top. Mum couldn't understand why I needed one. She said, "You must have about a hundred tops!"

I said, "Yes, but they're all old."

"*Old?*" Mum almost slammed the car into the gatepost. "You bought two only last month!"

"I've already worn those," I said. "They've already been seen."

"Well, it's your money," said Mum.

It was my birthday money that I'd been saving up. I was going to put it with my Christmas money – if I got any! – and buy a workstation for my bedroom. I'd wanted a workstation for ages. Now, suddenly, it seemed more important to have a new top. As I pointed out to Mum, it would hardly make any dent at all in my savings. And who knew? Maybe Mum and Dad might buy me a workstation! (I didn't say this bit to Mum, natch. But I'd hinted at it often enough!)

"I suppose you want to impress your friends," said Mum. "It's only natural. But I don't want you getting like Keri!" she added.

No danger of that. I couldn't afford it! I said this to Mum and she made a grumping noise that sounded like a cow blowing down its nostrils. "Hmph!" Like she thought Keri got far too much spending money and spent far too much of it on clothes. But it's nice to look cool! It makes you feel good. I said this to Mum, and she agreed that the way you look is important. "So long as it doesn't become an obsession."

All this, just because I wanted a new top! I said to Mum, "One top is not an obsession."

"No," said Mum, "but a dozen is coming perilously close!" And then she rolled her eyes and said, "If you're like this now, I dread to think how it's going to be when boys are on the scene!"

I assured Mum that this was not going to happen. "We are not into boys," I said.

"Give it a few months," said Mum.

"Give it a few *centuries*," I said.

Mum laughed. "I shall remind you of that!" she said.

Ha ha! She won't get the chance.

We went into this shop called Hot Spot to look for my top. It is not as classy as Go Girl but it is quite cool. I mean, you don't feel ashamed walking round with a bag that says Hot Spot on it. Not like Marks & Spencer! I just nearly died one time when Mum got some stuff from there and gave me the bag to carry and we bumped into Katie and Chantal. I could see their eyes, like, *boring* through the plastic, trying to suss out what was in there. Afterwards, I whinged at Mum about it and she told me not to be so silly. "All the best people shop at Marks & Sparks. Even the Queen!"

I bet Keri doesn't. I bet Keri wouldn't be seen dead in there!

Anyway, I found this really groovy top, bright red and sort of see-through. Well, almost see-through.

Mum wouldn't have let me have it if it had really been; she's not in he least bit cool. As for Dad, he's prehistoric! He'd have a fit. Mum wasn't too happy about it even as it was. She kept saying things like, "You'll need something underneath" or "Surely you ought to have something warmer?"

I said, "*Mum!* No one goes to parties in something warm!"

So in the end she let me buy it, and then I caught sight of this totally brilliant skirt, raspberry red with an enormous silver pocket shaped like a heart, and I just had to have it! I mean, I *could not* have walked out of the shop without it! Then I saw some tights that went with it, super-soft and stripey, in red and silver.

I said, "Mum, I need them! I haven't got anything else that would go!"

It made rather a large hole in my savings, but I was almost sure that Mum and Dad were going to get me a workstation for Christmas. I mean, what else could they get me? I didn't want anything else! Not anything big. And I'd been talking about a workstation for simply ages. In any case, you can't go to a party wearing stuff you've already worn a thousand times before. Not when people like Chantal are going to be there. And that horrible Jessamy. Like if she'd seen the Marks & Spencer bag it would have been all round the school in no time.

"Polly Roberts goes to Marks & Spencer!"

"Polly Roberts wears Marks & Spencer knickers!"

Being at the High School hadn't improved her one little bit. She was just as hateful as she's always been.

I spent ages getting ready for the party. I washed my hair in special shampoo from the Body Shop and then I did it in this really cool style I'd seen in a magazine. Well, as best I could, having short hair. What I did, I took two bits from the sides and one bit from the top and twizzled them round and fixed them with a glittery tinsel clip (like the one Keri had). I was really pleased when I looked at myself in the mirror, but then I got downstairs and Craig had to go and ruin it all. This is something he does to me ALL THE TIME.

"Ho ho ho, and what are you going as?" he said. "A Christmas tree?"

I really do *hate* boys.

"Craig, leave your sister alone," said Mum.

"Well, what's with all this—" Craig made twiddly motions with his fingers. "All this ravioli stuff on top of her head?"

I shouted, "That's a *hairstyle*, you blithering idiot!"

"Yes, and it looks very nice," said Mum.

"Almost good enough to eat ," said Dad.

Was he being funny??? Craig obviously thought so. He went off into his great honking laugh that he does. *Hee-honk, hee-honk*. Like some sort of human donkey.

"Craig! Out!" said Mum. And she shooed Craig out of the room and gave Dad this little frown and shake of the head. Dad at once sat up, all straight and serious, and said, "My pleasure, Mamzelle! May I have this dance?" He then added that I looked very pretty and he was sure that all the boys would go for me.

I snapped, "There aren't going to be any boys!"

"That's a pity," said Dad.

I didn't think it was a pity, and I don't think Mum did, either. She didn't want me going out with boys! She said, "Come on, Pol! Take no notice of them. Let's make a move."

It was a rotten, *rotten* party. I hated it! Katie hadn't just invited people from school, she'd invited

- the people that lived next door
- people that lived in her road
- people she'd met on holiday
- a whole bunch of cousins.

One of the people that lived next door plus one of

the people that lived in her road plus three of her cousins were boys. One of the boys was all right. He was called Jack and he was only little. He was about nine. All the others were big. There was one that was called Tristram that was utterly foul. He was thirteen and kept strutting about and making these really stupid remarks that everyone tittered at. Everyone except *me*.

All the other girls started flirting and showing off, trying to impress him. Even Chantal, that I would have thought better of. I mean, her being so cool and all. Even Chloë giggled and made her eyes go big whenever he looked in her direction. I just turned bright red like a nasturtium. Beverley saw me and cried, "Ooh, look! Polly's blushing!" So then of course, I blushed even more. I blushed furiously all over until I ended up the same colour as my lovely new top – which I now wished I hadn't worn. It wasn't *quite* see-through, but it was nearly. I didn't know there were going to be boys!

The worst part was when they played this stupid kissing game and we all had to keep going in and out of the room, and being kissed, and sitting on boys' laps. It was just so yucky! Then there was dancing, and someone, I think it was Katie, yelled, "Hey, Polly!

You're the littlest. Dance with Jack!" I had to do it 'cos I wouldn't have wanted to hurt his feelings, but everyone laughed and Chantal crooned, "Aaah! Sweet!" which made me go bright red all over again.

I spent most of the time all boiled up like a beetroot. When I wasn't doing that I was stuck in the bathroom, trying not to cry. I hated boys! I hated this party! Why had I come? I could have been with Frizz, all cosy and happy, eating her sicky pudding.

Thinking of Frizz made me feel bad. She was my *oldest* friend, she was my *best* friend. And I had let her down! I'd come to this horrible party just because Katie was popular and I wanted to be with the in-crowd. And now I was with them and I wasn't enjoying it one little bit. I wanted to go home!

I crept back downstairs from the bathroom, hoping that no one would see me, but Jessamy immediately shrieked, "There's Polly! Where have you been? Your boyfriend's pining for you!" And she grabbed hold of Jack and practically *thrust* him at me. It was so unfair! He was only nine. You shouldn't treat a poor little nine-year-old boy like that. I mean, it was really embarrassing for him.

"I think they're all mad," I said to him.

I did! I really did! They weren't behaving normally

at all. Even Bev, who at school is quite quiet and sensible, was all crazed and panting and batting her eyelids. Even Chloë. She came over to me at one point and giggled, "Have you seen Jessamy? She is absolutely hyper!"

Then she squeezed my arm and whispered, "We can talk it all over tomorrow!" and went twirling off again across the room. It seemed to me that Chloë was pretty hyper herself. I couldn't get over the way she had changed! All gooey and drippy, just because of boys.

Jack, standing next to me, said, "I don't like parties."

"Nor do I," I said. I'd thought I did. I'd been really looking forward to this one. I'd thought we'd, like, play games and eat tea and listen to music, maybe watch a video. I hadn't known it was going to be like this!

I was so relieved when Mum came to fetch me. I couldn't wait to snatch up my coat and rush out to the car.

"So how was it?" said Mum. "Was it a good party?"

"Boys," I mumbled.

"Boys?" Mum threw up her hands. "It's started!"

"Nothing has *started*,' I muttered. I was in quite a mean mood, to tell the truth, what with feeling guilty about Frizz and wishing I hadn't gone to the rotten party in the first place.

"Ah, well," said Mum. "We live and learn. What do you want for tea tomorrow?"

I must have looked blank, 'cos she said, "Tomorrow! When Chloë comes."

"I'm thinking about that," I said. "I might ask her to come next Sunday, instead... I might go round and see Frizz."

"Polly!" Mum looked at me, reproachfully. "You really can't keep messing people around like this!"

"Frizz is the only one I've messed around," I said. "I think I'll ring her and say that I can see her tomorrow after all."

"On your own head be it," said Mum. "Just don't be surprised if she doesn't want to see you."

"Why shouldn't she?" I said.

"Polly," said Mum, "even Dawn has her pride."

I frowned, and picked at a loose thread in my lovely stripey tights.

"How would you feel," said Mum, "if Dawn had let *you* down at the last minute, then suddenly rings up, all gracious, to say that she can manage to fit you in after all? You might not want to be fitted in, might you? You might feel that it was a bit...patronising?"

"I just want to see her!" I said.

First thing I did, soon as I got in, was ring Frizz's number.

"Hey, Frizz!" I said.

"Polly?" she said.

She didn't sound mad at me. She sounded... Frizz-like. Sort of eager, but anxious, both at the same time.

"Today has been *horrible*," I said. "I hated it! I'd far rather have been with you."

"Really?" said Frizz.

"Really really!" I said. Then there was a bit of a pause, during which I could almost feel Frizz blossoming at the other end of the line. I said, "Have you eaten your pudding yet?"

Frizz gave a little giggle. "Not yet! We were going to have it tonight."

"Don't!" I yelped. "Keep it for tomorrow!"

"T-tomorrow?" said Frizz. "W-why?"

"'Cos I want some," I said.

"But I thought you couldn't come tomorrow?" said Frizz.

"I can now," I said. "If you still want me to," I added, thinking about Frizz's pride and how she might have decided that she had better things to do. "Is it all right?" I said, humbly.

"*Yes!*" Frizz practically beamed at me down the telephone. "I'll make a special sauce to go with it!"

"So what's happening?" said Mum, as I went out to the kitchen. "Just so I know where we're at."

"I'm going to see Frizz," I said. "She wants me to. We're going to eat her pudding that she made. It's not that she hasn't any pride," I said to Mum. "It's just that she doesn't bear grudges."

"Well, you'd better go and ring Chloë and hope that she doesn't bear them, either," said Mum. "I'll tell you what, my girl! I'm going to get you a diary for your Christmas present!"

"A diary to go in my workstation!" I cried. I wasn't ever going to get into this sort of muddle again. I knew that I was really lucky to have a friend like Frizz, so funny, and so generous, and so good-natured. Someone who didn't bear grudges or stand on her pride. Who still wanted me to go round and share her pudding!

Sometimes I truly believe that Frizz is the *nicest* one out of the four of us.

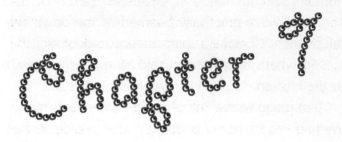

Chapter 7

I really didn't want to ring Chloë. I really didn't! But I knew that I had to; it wasn't any use expecting Mum to do it for me. Mum was quite cross, as a matter of fact. She kept saying how bad it was to let people down, and how would I like it if they did it to me?

"Have you rung yet?" she said, as we sat down to watch television.

"Not yet," I said.

"Why not?" said Mum. "What are you waiting for? You get out there and do it!"

So I trailed out into the hall and picked up the

receiver and dialled Chloë's number, and all the time I'm, like, having the collywobbles in the pit of my stomach, 'cos suppose Chloë says she's got something else to do next Sunday? Suppose she's sick of me, she doesn't want to be friends with me any more? Suppose, suppose…

She probably wouldn't want to be friends with me after the way I behaved at the party. Hiding in the bathroom like a total twonk! I was beginning to feel a bit ashamed of myself. Everyone else seemed to know how to behave with boys. Why didn't I???

And then someone picked up the phone, and it was Chloë, and I babbled about how I couldn't see her tomorrow after all, and she wasn't in the least bit cross! She said that in fact the following Sunday would be heaps better as her auntie and uncle were going to be there tomorrow afternoon, and she would quite like to see them. So *that* was all right. Hooray!

We then discussed the party. We agreed that Jessamy had been hyper, and that Tristram thought rather too much of himself, and that boys in general were quite gruesome.

"Except for Jack," said Chloë. "He was sweet!"

I said, "They are, when they're little. It's when they get bigger they're such a pain."

Chloë wanted to know if Craig was a pain. I said, "You'd better believe it!"

She giggled at this. She said, "Will he be there, when I come round?"

"Not if I can help it,' I said.

I felt good after speaking to Chloë. She still wanted to be my friend! She didn't seem to have noticed that I'd behaved oddly at the party. She didn't know that I had gone to hide in the bathroom. And she agreed with me that boys were a pain! I suddenly came over all bold and masterful. Instead of going back to watch television, I rang Keri. I said, "What are you doing tomorrow afternoon?"

Promptly she said, "Going skating. Why?"

I told her about Frizz, and about the pudding she'd made, and the special sauce, and how we'd all let her down.

"So I thought I'd go round tomorrow," I said. "But it's far too much for just the two of us."

"What sort of pudding is it?" said Keri.

"Fudge, I think. And she's making this sauce! It sounds really yummy."

"Really *yucky*."

"But she did it specially! The pudding. 'Cos she thought we were going to be there. She was ever so upset when I said I couldn't go."

"Why couldn't you?"

"'Cos I had to go to this party."

"Party?" Keri brightened. She adores parties! "Whose was it? Was it good?"

I said, "It was this girl at school's and it was all right except that there were boys there."

"Boys," said Keri. "Uh ho!"

"Boys ugh pooh," I said. "They ruin things."

"Yes. Well. I suppose," said Keri.

"They do! They're stupid! I wished I'd gone to Frizz's, instead."

"So you're going tomorrow?"

I said, "Yes, and I thought it would be really nice if we all did. 'Cos I think Frizz *deserves* it.'

There was a bit of a pause, then Keri said, "I suppose I'll have to go skating in the morning, then."

"I should think it would be better in the morning," I said.

"Well, it's not," said Keri. "I have friends there in the afternoon. One of them goes to my school. We travel back together. Now I'll have to go back by myself. I hate going back by myself! I wouldn't do it for anyone else," she said. "Only for Frizz!"

As soon as I said goodbye to Keri, I rang Lily.

"What are you doing tomorrow afternoon?" I said.

"Preparing ballet shoes," said Lily. "We're going on our points!"

She was very excited about going on her points. It seems it is a big thing in the life of a dancer. You're not allowed to do it until your feet are strong enough, and even then you have to wear special blocked shoes and your toes bleed so that you are in total and utter agony, but Lily was looking forward to it. She burbled about sewing on ribbons, like it was going to take all afternoon.

"Anyway," she said. "Why?"

I told her what I'd told Keri, except I didn't say about the pudding being yummy fudge, or about the special sauce that Frizz was doing to go with it.

"It would make her so happy," I said.

"Yes, and I have been a bit naughty just recently, haven't I?" said Lily. "Going off to all these classes."

"Well, I know it's important to you," I said.

"It is," agreed Lily, "but so's Frizz. What time d'you want us to get there?"

We arranged that we would all meet up at half past two.

"*Outside*. So we can surprise her!"

Frizz's eyes as she opened the door and found us there! They grew as big as dinner plates.

"Oh!" She clapped her hands to her cheeks. "You've all come!"

"We've come to eat the pudding," said Keri.

"Oh! The pudding!" Frizz giggled. "I've done a special sauce...it's really scrummy!"

"It had better be," said Keri. "I've been skating all morning and I'm *starving*."

"Why? Didn't you eat any lunch?" said Lily.

"Yes, but I left a hole for the pudding 'cos Polly told me about it. She said it sounded really *sickola*. Yum yum!"

Lily was beginning to look a bit stressed. She tugged anxiously at Keri's sleeve as we followed Frizz up the stairs. Keri just scowled at her and dragged her arm away. I scurried on, after Frizz.

"I didn't think you and me would be able to eat it all," I hissed.

Frizz giggled again. "Not without feeling ill!"

We all sat around in Frizz's room for a bit, exchanging gossip. Stuff that had happened at school. Things we'd done. Lily told us about going on her points, and about how her toes were going to bleed.

Keri told us about spending the weekend with her friend that had the pony, and how she was going to start riding lessons. Frizz told us about an extremely obnoxious boy called Vinny Hassett that used to be at Juniors with us and was now at Heathfield. Vinny Hassett had been caught trying to break into school through a lavatory window.

"He got stuck," gurgled Frizz. "Someone found him there and rang the police."

We all thought that was a really good story! Frizz looked pleased.

"Serves him right," said Lily. "He was always horrible."

Keri turned to me.

"Tell them about your party," she said. "The one with boys."

"Party?" said Frizz. "You went to a party?"

"It was a school thing," I said, hurriedly. "I couldn't get out of it. But it was really draggy! It's too boring to talk about."

Frizz opened her mouth. I could see she was going to start asking questions, wanting to know whose party it was and why I hadn't been able to get out of it and why I hadn't told her. So very quickly I sprang up and cried, "Pudding time!"

"Yes!" Keri beat on the floor with her fist. "Where's the pudding? I want pudding!"

Frizz beamed. "You stay there and I'll go and get it."

We heard her footsteps thudding down the stairs. Lily, at once, scrambled to her feet.

"Listen, you guys! I can't eat fudge pudding, I'm going on my points tomorrow!"

"A little bit isn't going to make any difference," said Keri.

"It is! It would! It's deadly! I'll get fat as fat!"

"On one little bit of fudge pudding?"

"Honestly!" Lily looked at us, beseechingly. She has these enormous dark eyes in this tiny elfin face. Like a spider monkey, my dad once said. "Miss Banks always says you can tell *immediately* if someone's been on a binge!"

"I don't call one little bit of fudge pudding going on a binge," said Keri.

"Just one little itsy bitsy tiny little piece," I pleaded. "'Cos of Frizz making it specially. A little itsy bitsy piece." I held my finger and thumb about a centimetre apart. "That wouldn't hurt? Would it?"

Lily had got that stubborn expression she sometimes gets. Not very often; but just now and again. She digs her heels in and you can't budge her.

We heard Frizz's footsteps clumping back up the stairs.

"Just one little itsy bitsy piece," I crooned. "Dear, sweet Lily...couldn't you?"

"Yes! She could!" Keri suddenly jumped up and went marching over to Lily. Lily's expression change to one of alarm. Keri is the tallest and biggest of us. She is quite muscly. (From all the skating that she does and the hockey that she plays.) Lily is way the smallest and skinny as a piece of thread.

"We are *all* going to eat some of Frizz's pudding," hissed Keri. "Even you! Just one *tiny little piece.*"

Lily stammered, "B-but—"

"We're her *friends*,' said Keri. "This is what friends *do*.'

I thought, "What, eat fudge pudding?" and nearly giggled. Except that I didn't 'cos Keri was being dead serious.

"They *stand by* each other," said Keri. "They *stick up* for each other. This is Frizz's thing... She's made us a *pudding*. So we're going to *eat* it. Right?"

"Right! Right!" Lily nodded. "For Frizz...right!" Then she turned to me and whispered, "I can always eat nothing but salad tomorrow."

"Of course you can," I said.

"After all, it is for Frizz."

"Well, this is it," I said.

Lily beamed. "So I don't really mind!"

"OK, you guys!" The door burst open and Frizz came in, beaming broadly with a tray. "Fudge pudding!"

She began to plonk bits on to our plates.

"A *big* bit for Keri, 'cos she's not on a diet any more...a *big* bit for me, 'cos I've never been on a diet...a *big* bit for Polly, 'cos she doesn't need to go on a diet, and a *small* bit for Lily 'cos she's *always* on a diet!"

"Where's the sauce?" demanded Keri. "I want sauce!"

The sauce was chocolate, very thick and gluggy. I could see Lily practically quaking in her shoes, but Frizz was kind to her. Frizz can surprise you sometimes.

"I don't think Lily ought to have any of this," she said. "Not if she's going on her points. It'll make her top heavy. And anyway, it's more for the rest of us!"

"Oh, and it looks *so* good," said Lily.

Keri assured her that it was. "It's really scrummy!"

She was right. It was the yummiest, scrummiest pudding and the gluggiest, creamiest sauce I have ever tasted!

"I'm glad you're enjoying it," said Frizz. She had

sauce smeared all over her chin!

"It's more than just enjoying it," said Keri. "This is an experience, man!"

Frizz's cheeks grew hot and pink with pleasure.

Very somemnly, Keri held out her spoon, heaped high with pudding.

"To friends," she said.

We all held out our spoons. "To friends!"

The Gang of Four...Lily 'n' Keri 'n' Frizzle 'n' me. We'd vowed to stick together, and we had!

Hooray!

About the Author

Jean Ure had her first book published while she was still at school and immediately went rushing out into the world declaring that she was AN AUTHOR. But it was another few years before she had her second book published, and during that time she had to work at lots of different jobs to earn money. In the end she went to drama school to train as an actress. While she was there she met her husband and wrote another book. She has now written more than eighty books! She lives in Croydon with her husband and their family of seven rescued dogs and four rescued cats.

Girlfriends

Find out whether the Gang of Four stay friends for ever in the next book in the series!

Girlfriends

Girls Are Groovy!

JEAN URE

978 1 84616 962 5 £4.99

Chapter 1

I was upstairs in my bedroom, rolling about with Bundle (he's my dog) when Mum called up to me. "Pollee! Keri's on the phone!"

I said, "Keri?" Keri doesn't ring me all that often. It's usually me and Frizz that ring each other.

I charged downstairs and snatched up the phone. "Keri?" I said. "Hi!"

"Hi," said Keri. "Want to come to a party?"

"Ooh, yes, please!" I said. I love parties. "Is it a New Year's one?"

"Yes. It's a pool party. To celebrate our pool."

I knew about Keri's pool. Well, her mum and dad's pool, really. The reason I knew was that my dad was the one who had put it in! It's what he does, he puts pools in for people. But he doesn't very often put them *inside* their houses! They're mostly outside in the garden and would probably be fre-e-e-ezing on New Year's Eve. But Keri's mum and dad are simply stupendously rich, and this is the sort of thing that you can do when you are rich...have heated pools inside your house! If ever I am rich that is what I am going to do. And I am going to swim in it morning and night and three times on a Sunday. I can think of nothing more blissful!

"We've got a sauna, as well," said Keri. "And a jacuzzi."

"Is that one of those things you whizz round in?" I said.

"Yes, but it's not working properly yet. When it is you can all come over and we'll whizz round like crazy! New Year's is just for the pool. Your mum and dad are invited, too, natch! Your dad's here right now. Mum's just asked him."

"Did he say yes?" I said. You never know, with Dad. Sometimes Mum complains he's a bit of a stay-at-home. But Keri said he'd promised he and Mum would go, so that was all right. Hooray! What a fab place to hold a party...in a pool!

Read the rest of

Girls Are Groovy!

to find out what happens next...

Pink knickers aren't cool!

Neither is Jessamy James, their owner. Nor is going to secondary school...especially if the gang of four have to split up! But bad boys and bad underwear are nothing compared with the problems facing Polly and the girlfriends' future.

Can they stick together, or will they end up being torn apart?

£4.99   978 1 84616 961 8

£4.99   978 1 84616 964 9

The girlfriends are growing up
and entering a whole new world, and boys
are a major part of it.

After their separate summer holidays, Polly is
alarmed when her friends start showing an
interest in boys, but is even more alarmed when
boys start showing an interest in her!

Reluctant to grow up, will Polly be left behind?
Or will she realise that not all boys are
what they seem...?

Girlfriends

More Orchard Red Apples

❑ Pink Knickers Aren't Cool!	*Jean Ure*	978 1 84616 961
❑ Girls Stick Together!	*Jean Ure*	978 1 84616 963
❑ Girls Are Groovy!	*Jean Ure*	978 1 84616 962
❑ Boys Are OK!	*Jean Ure*	978 1 84616 964
❑ Do Not Read This Book	*Pat Moon*	978 1 84121 435
❑ Do Not Read Any Further	*Pat Moon*	978 1 84121 456
❑ Do Not Read Or Else!	*Pat Moon*	978 1 84616 082
❑ The Shooting Star	*Rose Impey*	978 1 84362 56
❑ My Scary Fairy Godmother	*Rose Impey*	978 1 84362 68
❑ Hothouse Flower	*Rose Impey*	978 1 84616 21
❑ Introducing Scarlett Lee	*Rose Impey*	978 1 84616 70
❑ The Truth About Josie Green	*Belinda Hollyer*	978 1 84362 88
❑ Secrets, Lies & My Sister Kate	*Belinda Hollyer*	978 1 84616 69

All priced at £4.99 apart from those marked * which are £5.99.
Orchard Red Apples are available from all good bookshops,
or can be ordered direct from the publisher:
Orchard Books, PO BOX 29, Douglas IM99 1BQ
Credit card orders please telephone 01624 836000
or fax 01624 837033
or e-mail: bookshop@enterprise.net for details.

To order please quote title, author and ISBN
and your full name and address.
Cheques and postal orders should be made payable to 'Bookpost plc.'
Postage and packing is FREE within the UK
(overseas customers should add £1.00 per book).

Prices and availability are subject to change.

BL: 4.0